Charles M. Schulz

Leaf It to Sally Brown

BONK!

HarperHorizon
An Imprint of HarperCollins*Publishers*

First published in 1998 by HarperCollins*Publishers* Inc. http://www.harpercollins.com. Copyright © 1998 United Feature Syndicate, Inc. All rights reserved. HarperCollins ® and ® are trademarks of HarperCollins*Publishers* Inc. *Leaf It to Sally Brown* was published by HarperHorizon, an imprint of HarperCollins*Publishers* Inc., 10 East 53rd Street, New York, NY 10022. Horizon is a registered trademark used under license from Forbes Inc. PEANUTS is a registered trademark of United Feature Syndicate, Inc. PEANUTS © United Feature Syndicate, Inc. Based on the PEANUTS® comic strip by Charles M. Schulz. http://www.unitedmedia.com. ISBN 0-694-01030-8. Printed in China.

"I hate these field trips!"

"What are we supposed to be doing, anyway?"

"What are we supposed to be taking notes on, Linus?"

"Trees . . . we're supposed to
write down the names of all
the different trees we see."

"How many trees have you written down, Linus?"

"Oak, poplar, spruce, apple, maple, pine, cedar, and birch. That makes eight."

"I hate studying trees! What do I care about trees?"

"You shouldn't say bad things about trees, Sally."

"Why? What can a tree do to you?"

"I'm going to take this leaf to school for my report on trees, big brother. What do you think I should say about it?"

"You could talk about how we all feel sort of sad when the leaves begin to fall."

"I should feel sad because a leaf fell?"

"Well, describe to them how you felt when you saw the leaf fall from the tree."

"Tell how you felt seeing it drift
down to earth for the last time."

"I found it in the driveway."

"This is my report on our field trip
among the trees."

"First, we boarded the bus that took us for a ride that was the most miserable, boring, sickening, painful, uncomfortable . . ."

"Okay, about the trees . . ."

"Some people think when leaves begin to fall, it is the saddest time of year. They're wrong."

"The saddest time of year is your birthday when you don't get any of the things you wanted. Ma'am?"

"Okay, about this stupid leaf . . ."

"Well, so much for another miserable 'show and tell.'"